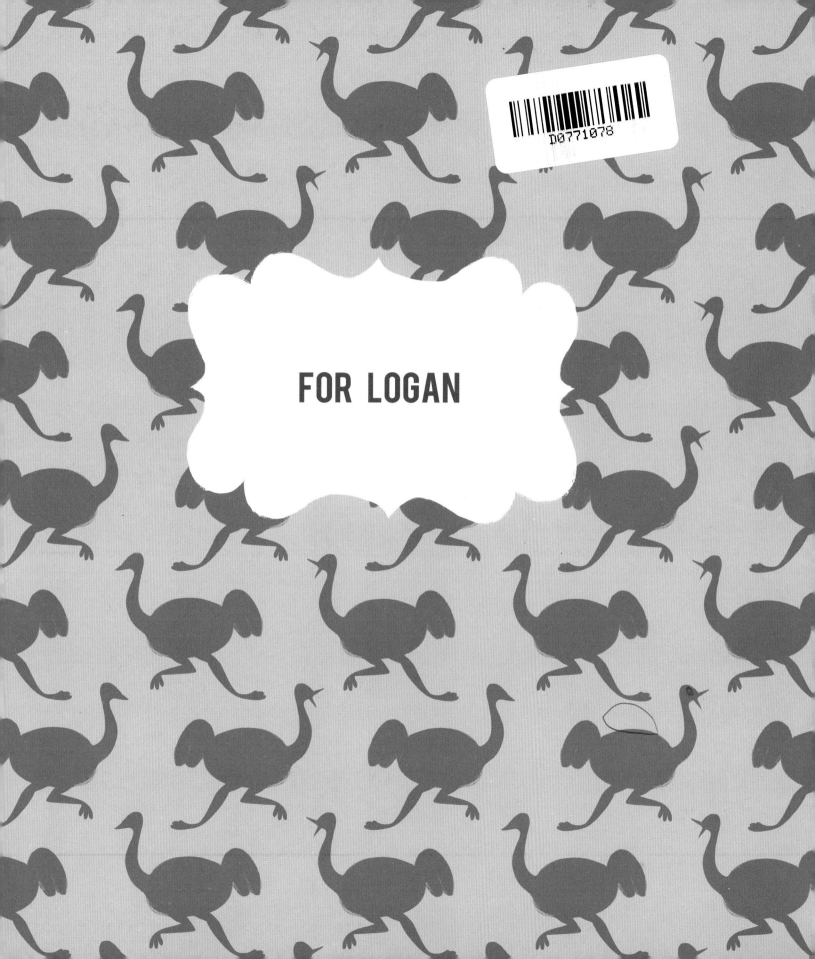

FOR LOGAN

Kids! Abby's here!
We're headed out. You
two be good.

# THE Night OUR PARENTS WENT OUT

WRITTEN BY
**KATiE GOODMAN**
AND **SOREN KiSiEL**

iLLUSTRATED BY
**CAT TUONG BUi**

**POW!**

**BROOKLYN, NY**

Are they coming back?

Will they be okay?

Of course! It's just a date night—before you were born, they used to do this all the time. They're going to have dinner, see a movie and maybe get some dessert. They'll be home before you know it!

But what if something happens?!

What could happen?

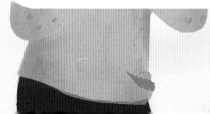

There could be a hot air balloon taking off from the restaurant parking lot, and if Dad got his foot caught in the ropes and Mom tried to grab him, they might get so high up that they can't see anything but clouds!

And **unicorns!**

Unicorns can't fly.

Duh! They ride on rainbows! And they might pop the balloon with their horns!

Then they'd be EVIL unicorns!

Oh no! Mom and Dad are up there with evil unicorns!!

Come on, guys—your parents can handle this! All hot-air balloons have sandbags, right? And rainbows can't hold a lot of weight, can they? I bet your mom and dad would grab a few of those sandbags, jump on the back of a unicorn and  . . .

Unicorn-elevator, going down!

But then what if Dad orders the squid for dinner, and it escapes from the kitchen?
And it comes slithering into the dining room!
Because the chef accidentally got a GIANT squid!!
And it's mad 'cause it doesn't want to be dinner!

Your mom would just braid those tentacles right up!
She's really good at braids!
And they can hold the braids together with her ponytail scrunchie!

But what if it turns out that at the movie theater the usher who takes their ticket is a vampire?
And that's why he likes to work in the dark!
And Dad accidentally gets a paper cut from the movie ticket and it starts bleeding and it's just too much for the vampire to resist?!

POP!
POPCORN
POP!
POP!
Well that sounds like something a bandage could take care of.
Too late—the vampire usher has already seen the blood!
Well then, your mom and dad are going to have to start a pop-cano!
A what?!

THEATER 2

Your mom could jump behind the concession stand and jam the popcorn maker into the "On" position: now it's a popcorn volcano!

With rivers of molten butter flowing down the sides!

But what if it turns out that when Mom gets up and goes to the bathroom...
She steps in quicksand in the dark hallway?!
Because it's a jungle movie and they accidentally decorated the theater with quicksand instead of regular sand!
Your dad could pull her out.
But what if it's a quicksand monster, and it comes after them?

Well, everyone knows the best way to scare off a movie monster is with another monster, right?

But what if they go out for dessert, and order mini-cupcakes but the reason the cupcakes are so small is that the baker puts shrinking powder in them...
And when he made Mom's and Dad's cupcakes, he put in WAY too much, so when they ate them they shrank down to the size of crumbs?!
And even though they screamed, "HELP!" in teeny-tiny voices, the baker accidentally brushed them into the sink and down the drain!

SHRINKING POWDER
Where there are teeny-tiny sewer alligators!!
There are teeny-tiny alligators in the sewer?
From pouring leftover shrinking powder down the drain!

Well, your mom's wearing heels, which make great grappling hooks! I'm sure in no time at all they'd be up and out of that drain.
But how would they get big again?!
Have you ever had a jumbo-sized cookie?
I love them!

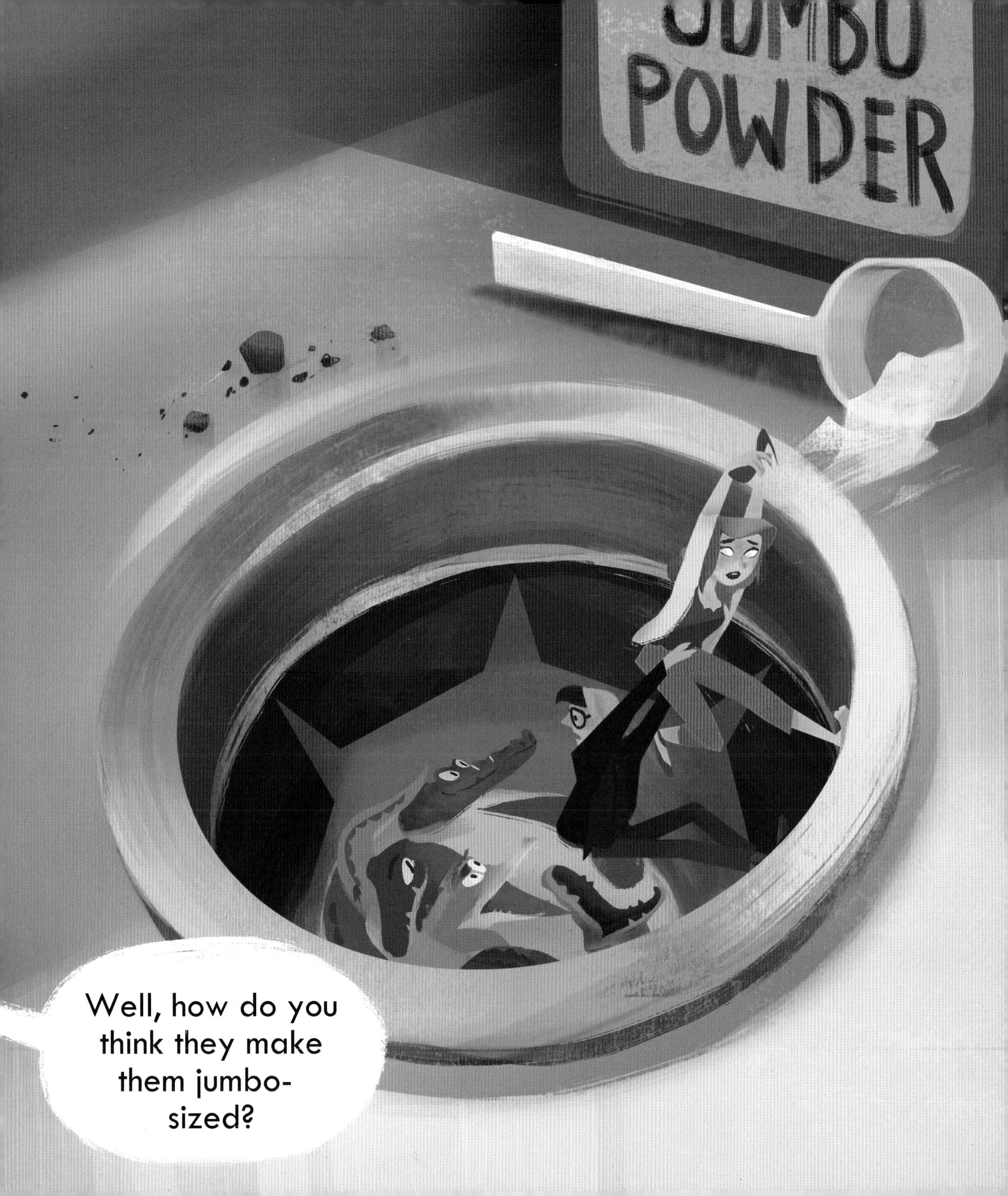
POWDER
Well, how do you think they make them jumbo-sized?

Ummmmm ... Well... I guess they'd use their jet—

We're home!

Thank you, Abby! See you next time.

Bye, kids!

Oh, and be careful on your way out not to trip over our new ostriches!

**The Night Our Parents Went Out**

© 2015 by Katie Goodman and Soren Kisiel
Illustrations © 2015 Cat Tuong Bui

Published in the United States by POW!
a division of powerHouse Packaging & Supply, Inc.
37 Main Street, Brooklyn, NY 11201-1021
telephone 718-801-8376
email info@POWkidsbooks.com

www.POWkidsbooks.com
www.powerHouseBooks.com
www.powerHousePackaging.com

Library of Congress Control Number: 2015946793

ISBN 9781576877470

10 9 8 7 6 5 4 3 2 1

Printed in Malaysia

With special thanks to
Brian DeFiore, Judith Viorst,
Kent Davis, Stuart Gibbs,
Randy Kaplan, Bill Fagerbakke,
Deb Shapiro, Deborah Sloan,
Krzysztof Poluchowicz,
Sharyn Rosart and
everyone at powerHouse.

And to our parents for teaching
us the magic of a tale well told.